Disgusting Denzil

Tessa Krailing

Illustrated by
Mike Phillips

OXFORD
UNIVERSITY PRESS

OXFORD
UNIVERSITY PRESS

Great Clarendon Street, Oxford, OX2 6DP,
United Kingdom

Oxford University Press is a department of the University of Oxford.
It furthers the University's objective of excellence in research, scholarship,
and education by publishing worldwide. Oxford is a registered trade mark of
Oxford University Press in the UK and in certain other countries

British Library Cataloguing in Publication Data
Data available

978-0-19-837715-3

1 3 5 7 9 10 8 6 4 2

Paper used in the production of this book is a natural, recyclable product
made from wood grown in sustainable forests. The manufacturing process
conforms to the environmental regulations of the country of origin.

Printed in China by Leo Paper Products Ltd.

Acknowledgements
Cover and inside illustrations by Mike Phillips
Inside cover notes written by Sasha Morton

Contents

Chapter 1

Everyone's Favourite Little Monster

"Oh, Denzil!" cried his mother, when he flicked chicken curry, SPLAT! over her best dress.

"Denzil, you are *disgusting!*" said his father, when he squirted tomato ketchup, WHOOSH! over the table.

They both smiled at him admiringly.

Denzil felt proud. He knew he was disgusting. People often told him so.

"Denzil, you're the most disgusting little monster in Monster City," they said.

Every morning he stared happily at himself in the mirror.

His hair was spiky, his nose ran and his mouth dribbled.

No wonder his mother and father adored him.

No wonder his
teacher, Miss Peabody,
gave him lots of
stars.

He was everyone's favourite little
monster.

Until the day when it all began to go
badly wrong.

It started like any other day, with
a really mucky, yucky breakfast.
Denzil managed to get it all over
everything.

"Good shot!" said Dad, taking a piece
of tomato from his left eye.

"Another winner!" said Mum. She picked
up the piece of toast he had dropped, jam
side down, on the floor.

Denzil smiled proudly.

Suddenly, Mum turned pale.

"Donovan …" she said. (Donovan was the name of Denzil's dad.) "Donovan, can you fetch my suitcase? Quickly, please!"

Denzil didn't ask why his mother wanted her suitcase in the middle of breakfast. He was too busy slurping up his milk. Slurp, slurp, guzzle, BURP!

"Did you hear that, Mum?" he boasted.

But his mother didn't tell him how clever he was, like she usually did. She just said, "Go to school, Denzil." She pushed him out of the house, without even kissing him goodbye.

Puzzled, he made his way to school.

There, to his relief, things got better
again. The first lesson was Mucky
Jokes. He told a joke about a monster
who sat on a plate of mouldy cheese.

The other little monsters fell about
laughing.

"Oh, Denzil," said Miss Peabody. "That
was the most disgusting joke I've ever
heard!" She gave him four red stars, the
highest mark you could get.

The rest of the day wasn't bad either. In the art lesson, they had to do a self-portrait.

"That means you have to paint yourself," explained Mr Boggis, the art teacher.

So Denzil painted himself all over in red and yellow stripes.

In the music lesson, he blew his nose so loudly that everyone thought there was an earthquake.

Yes, it was a very good day!

Until he went home and Dad told him he had a new baby sister.

Chapter 2
Devora

Her name was Devora.

Dad took Denzil to see her at the hospital. She lay in a cot beside Mum's bed.

"Come and look at her," said Mum. "Little Devora. Isn't she sweet?"

The baby had a bald head, a scarlet face, a blobby nose and screwed-up eyes. Yes, thought Denzil, she was rather sweet. But he wasn't going to say so.

Mum and Dad were gazing at her and making silly goo-goo noises.

"Who's Daddy's pride and joy, then?" cooed Dad.

Pride and joy? Denzil was shocked and hurt. That's what Dad had always called *him*. Yet the baby had done nothing to deserve such praise.

Nothing at all. It just lay there, like a – well, like a baby.

Suddenly she yawned – a yawn so enormous that Denzil stepped back hastily.

The baby's mouth was like a deep,
red cavern.

He had never seen a mouth so huge.
It seemed about twice the size of the rest of
her body. Yet, when she shut it again,
it looked quite normal.

"Give her to me," said Mum. "I want to
hold her."

Gently, Dad lifted the baby out of
the cot. He placed her in Mum's arms.
The baby opened her eyes and smiled. She
sicked up a whole lot of white stuff.

"What a clever girl!" cried Dad.
"I reckon she's going to be even more
disgusting than Denzil."

A cold, clammy fear took hold of
Denzil. He stared at his baby sister.

Devora dribbled and coughed. Then she
yawned again, showing her toothless gums
in an awesome display of disgustingness.
Was she really going to be worse than
him?

"Little Devora," said Mum, tenderly.

Chapter 3
"She Won't Hurt You"

From the moment Devora came home
from the hospital, Denzil's life changed.
The baby was all that anybody wanted to
look at.

"Isn't she amazing!" they cried. "Isn't
she gorgeous!"

Nobody took any notice of Denzil,
at all.

And Devora put on a real show for them. She was disgusting at the top end, forever dribbling and blowing raspberries. And she was even more disgusting at the bottom end. Well, it's probably better not to say what happened at the bottom end.

Even Denzil had to admit that it was far more disgusting than anything he could do.

"Denzil, would you like to hold your baby sister?" offered Mum.

"No thanks," he said.

"Go on, take her," said Mum. "She won't hurt you."

She put the baby into his arms.

Denzil stared down at Devora. Devora stared up at Denzil. Then she opened her mouth and screamed.

Now, when Devora screamed, it was worse than when she yawned.

She made the most terrible noise, and her mouth was so huge that you could see right down to her stomach. At least, that's how it seemed to Denzil.

And he was scared. He was so scared that he wanted to run away. Yet he couldn't. He just sat there, staring into the large red hole that was Devora's mouth.

Mum laughed. "Oh dear, I expect she's got a dirty nappy. You can help me change her."

Denzil was stunned into silence. When it came to disgustingness, Devora beat him every time.

How would he ever make people notice him again?

Chapter 4
Slugs and Slime and Slippery Fish

Denzil thought and thought.

He had to think of something brilliant. Something that would make Mum and Dad take notice of him again. At last he had an idea.

He went into the garden and collected the biggest, fattest, ooziest slugs that ever lurked under a stone.

Not snails, they weren't
disgusting enough. He took them
into the living room and tipped
them on to the carpet.

"Look what I've got," he said,
proudly.

No one bothered to look. They
were too busy gazing at Devora.
She was lying on a blanket,
kicking her legs and gurgling
wetly.

"LOOK WHAT I'VE GOT,"
said Denzil in a louder voice. "Slugs.
Masses of them. Lovely oozy,
snoozy, woozy slugs."

Mum glanced at them briefly. "Very nice," she said, and went back to admiring Devora.

"Look, Dad," said Denzil. "They're leaving a slimy trail all over the carpet."

"Mmm," said Dad, and went back to admiring Devora.

Denzil sighed sadly.

Then Devora saw a slug slithering across the carpet towards her. A look of wonder and delight came over her face. She waited until the slug came closer. Then, quick as a flash, her fat little hand shot out.

She grabbed it.

"Oh, look!" said Mum. "She likes them. Go and find her some more, Denzil."

Sadly, Denzil went back outside. His plan had failed. Once again, Devora had beaten him.

What next?

At the bottom of the garden was a pond. It was a truly mucky pond, full of weeds and stinking slime. Denzil drew a deep breath and waded in with all his clothes on.

Then he waded out again. He stood
on the bank, dripping wet and covered in
smelly green slime.

Disgusting!

Proudly, he went indoors. "Look at me.
I fell in the water," he said.

This wasn't true. But he didn't
want to admit that he had walked into the
pond on purpose.

Dad sniffed the air. "What's that lovely
pong?"

Denzil puffed out his chest. "It's me!" he
boasted.

"No, it's Devora," said Mum. "Her nappy needs changing again."

Denzil's shoulders sagged with disappointment.

At that moment, Devora saw him. She smiled and held out both her arms.

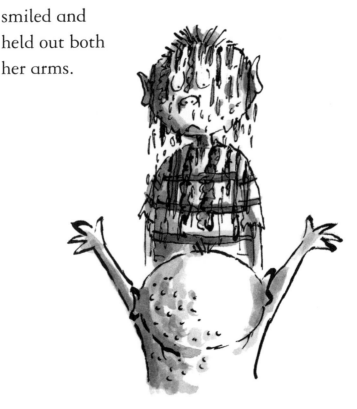

"Oh, the little love!" said Mum. "She wants you to pick her up, Denzil."

"I don't think it's Denzil she wants," said Dad. "It's that fish poking out of his pocket."

Denzil looked down. Sure enough, there was a large, slippery, slithery fish sticking out of his pocket. It must have got there while he was wading through the pond.

He pulled it out and stared at it.

Devora chuckled with delight. She got up from the floor and staggered towards him.

"Her first steps!" cried Mum.

"Give her the fish, Denzil," said Dad. "She deserves a reward."

But Denzil didn't have time to give her the fish. She had already snatched it out of his hands. Next moment, she opened her huge mouth. She dropped the slimy, slippery fish inside.

Then she snapped her mouth shut and swallowed hard.

GULP!
GULP!
GULP!
BURP!

Denzil couldn't speak. He had never felt so disgusted in his life.

"Her first real food!" cried Dad. "She's growing up fast. She'll be talking next."

Denzil's heart sank to the bottom of his squelchy boots. Every time he tried to be disgusting, Devora managed to be even more disgusting. It was hopeless. Nothing he could do would ever make his family admire him again.

Sadly, he turned around and walked out of the front door.

Nobody even saw him go.

Chapter 5
Little Treasure

Sadly, Denzil trudged along the street.

"Hello, Denzil," called out Mrs
Wart. "I hear you've got a new sister.
Congratulations!"

Denzil couldn't even manage a smile.
He shrugged and walked on.

"Hello, Denzil," called out Miss
Peabody, his teacher. "I hear your baby
sister's growing up fast. She'll soon be
ready to come to school."

Denzil opened his mouth to speak, but no sound came out. The thought of Devora coming to school was too awful. Bad enough having her grab all the attention at home, without having to compete with her at school as well.

He shrugged and walked on.

"Hi, Denzil!" called out Sickening Susan, who sat next to him in class. "You are lucky, having a new baby sister. I wish I had one."

"You can have mine," was what he
wanted to say. But he didn't. He just
shrugged and walked on. At last he came
to the park.

He sat down on a bench.

Two large tears rolled down his cheeks.
He was no longer the most disgusting little
monster in Monster City. Only the *brother*
of the most disgusting little monster in
Monster City.

Someone came to sit beside him. Denzil brushed away the tears. Mustn't let anyone see him crying.

Then he realized who it was: Boastful Bertha. She was holding on to a pram.

Not another baby! Denzil had had quite enough of babies, thanks very much. He got up to go.

"Look, Denzil," said Bertha. "This is my baby brother. Isn't he disgusting?"

Denzil glanced at the baby in the pram.
It looked a pretty boring sort of baby, he
thought.

"Not as disgusting as my baby sister,"
he said.

The baby sicked up something revolting
and green.

"Look at that," said Bertha. "He's been
eating grass. I bet your baby sister doesn't
eat grass."

"She eats fish," said Denzil. "Raw."

The baby screwed up his eyes and made a very rude noise.

"He's got wind," said Bertha. "I bet your baby sister doesn't make noises like that."

"When my baby sister has got wind," said Denzil, "everyone runs out in the street. They think there's a war going on."

The baby's face turned red. He opened his mouth and screamed.

"I bet your baby sister can't yell as loud as that," said Bertha.

"When my baby sister yells," said Denzil, "you can hear her a hundred miles away. And when she opens her mouth, it's so big you can see right down to her stomach. Her mouth is bigger than a shark's. I bet she could swallow a whole person if she wanted to."

Bertha stared at him. "That's impossible."

Denzil shrugged. "Come round to our house and have a look."

"When?"

"Now."

Denzil set off. Behind him, he heard the pram wheels squeaking as Bertha followed him home.

"Hello, Mum," he called out, as he opened the front door. "Can Boastful Bertha have a look at Devora?"

"Yes, of course," said Mum. "Is that your new baby brother, Bertha? My, isn't he disgusting!"

"He's not as disgusting as Devora," said Denzil. There was definitely a note of pride in his voice.

They entered the living room. A crowd stood around Devora, gazing at her admiringly. They made way for Denzil and Bertha, who was carrying her baby brother.

When Bertha's baby brother saw Devora, he opened his mouth and screamed.

Devora looked up in surprise.

Then she, too, opened her mouth and screamed.

Everyone drew back hastily, covering their ears. Bertha turned pale.

Bertha's baby brother stopped screaming. He clutched her tightly. Bertha stared down at Devora's huge mouth. It was getting bigger and bigger with every scream.

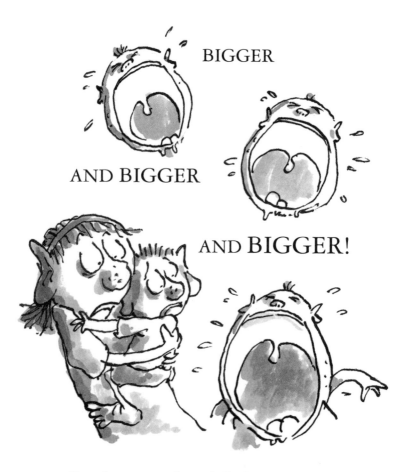

BIGGER

AND BIGGER

AND BIGGER!

Bertha turned and fled.

As soon as the other baby had gone, Devora stopped screaming. She closed her mouth and smiled. She looked up at Denzil and said in a hoarse, booming voice, "Den – zil."

Everyone gasped.

"Listen to that!" cried Dad. "Her first word."

"I knew it wouldn't be long before she started talking," said Mum. "The little love."

Denzil nearly burst with pride. Devora was far, far more disgusting than Bertha's baby brother. And her very first word had been his name.

"Den – zil," Devora said again, loudly and clearly. "Den – zil, Den – zil, Den – zil." She held out both hands, waggling her short fat fingers.

"Look at that," sighed everyone. "How she loves her big brother!"

Dad looked puzzled. "I think she wants something," he said.

Denzil smiled. "Slugs, I expect," he said. "The others have all wriggled away. I'll fetch her some more."

Happily, he picked up a cardboard box and went into the garden.

About the author

I've written stories ever since I can remember, but I was quite grown up before I had my first book published. That was about a dinosaur. Since then I've written about dogs, cats, snakes, iguanas and all kinds of creatures.

But I've never written about a monster before. So this is a story about a really, really disgusting little monster ...